Mike's Math Game

Jamie Holloway

Rosen
REAL
READERS

Rosen
Classroom™
New York

1

Mike does not likes math. He does not think it is so much fun.

He does his homework. He needs to spend 20 minutes. He spends 10 minutes on facts. He spends 10 minutes on a worksheet.

His dad asks him if he is OK. He looks kind of sad. Mike tells him he wishes math could be more fun.

His dad tells him that there is a way. He
goes and gets his laptop computer.

He searches for "fun math games"
online. He pulls up a site and signs Mike
up. He shows Mike how to log in.

Mike and his dad look at all the different math games he can play. They pick one that helps him remember his math facts.

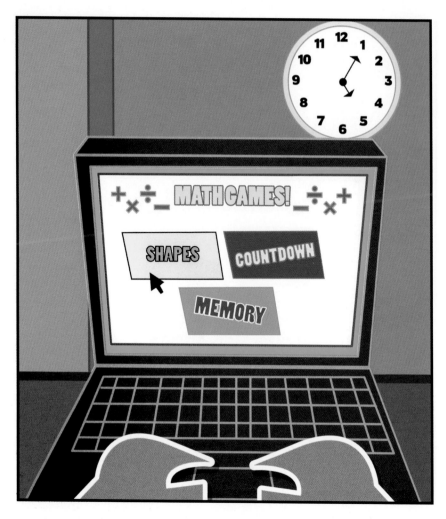

Mike plays it. It is fun! He plays the game for 15 minutes. Then he picks another game with shapes.

He plays that game for 15 minutes, too.

He has just done math for 30 minutes.

Math is now fun.

Mike does his regular math homework
every afternoon. He also uses the
computer to play math games. He
is better at math. He likes it more, too.

His dad shows Mike that he can
play games on many topics. There
are cool science games. There are
games for spelling and geography, too.

Mike is having fun learning while using his computer. He looks forward to new math questions in school. He likes to try out new math games!